Emma Barnes

How (Not) To Make Bad Children Good

Emma Barnes

illustrated by Emma Chichester Clark

www.stridentpublishing.co.uk

Published by
Strident Publishing Ltd
22 Strathwhillan Drive
The Orchard, Hairmyres
East Kilbride G75 8GT

Tel: +44 (0)1355 220588
info@stridentpublishing.co.uk
www.stridentpublishing.co.uk

Published by Strident Publishing Limited, 2011
Text © Emma Barnes, 2011
Cover and interior illustrations © Emma Chichester Clark, 2011

A catalogue record for this book is
available from the British Library.

ISBN 978-1-905537-28-0

Typeset in Baskerville by lawrencemann.co.uk
Printed by Cox & Wyman

Also by

Emma Barnes

Jessica Haggerthwaite: Witch Dispatcher

ISBN: 978-1-905537-30-3 (paperback, RRP £6.99)

Jessica has always planned to be a world-famous scientist one day. But now her mother has become a professional witch!

Who will take Jessica seriously now?

To stop her mother wrecking her plans (and breaking up the family), Jessica resolves to show her that no one needs to believe in magic these days. But her plans – like her mother's spells – don't always have the desired effect...

www.stridentpublishing.co.uk

Emma Chichester Clark

Emma studied at the Chelsea School of Art and the Royal College, where she was taught by Quentin Blake. Her first book, Listen To This!, won the 1988 Mother Goose Award for best newcomer to children's book illustration.

She has illustrated books by Roald Dahl, Kevin Crossley-Holland and Michael Morpurgo, as well as writing and illustrating many of her own books, including I Love You Blue Kangaroo, which has won awards in Italy and the USA, and was shortlisted for the Kate Greenaway Medal. Melrose And Croc Together At Christmas was a finalist in the Blue Peter Book Awards.

Her most recent books include Hansel And Gretel, a collaboration with Michael Morpurgo, and Alice In Wonderland, nominated for the 2011 Kate Greenaway Medal.

Emma Barnes

Emma grew up in Edinburgh, studied at Cambridge and now lives in Leeds. Her first novel, Jessica Haggerthwaite: Witch Dispatcher, was shortlisted for the Branford Boase Award and led to her being compared to Roald Dahl and Jacqueline Wilson.

Her books have been translated into several languages and broadcast on BBC Radio. She regularly visits schools, festivals and libraries, sharing her passion for books and reading. If you would like to contact her to discuss a visit please email EmmaJBarnes@yahoo.co.uk or visit her web-site: www.EmmaBarnes.info

Acknowledgements

With a Big Thank You
to
Abigail, Bonnie, Laura, Luke, Piyusha and Zack
All of them Good, Not Bad

CHAPTER ONE
A New Challenge

Martha Bones was in trouble again.

"Bed! This moment!" yelled Mum.

"And don't come down!" yelled Dad.

"But it's not my fault!" shrieked Martha. "It was an ACCIDENT!"

"We don't want to hear!" they yelled.

Martha stormed up the stairs.

It wasn't fair, she thought. Anybody could accidentally drop their sister's library book down the toilet. And then pull the flush. Anybody could accidentally write *Baby For Sale* across their baby brother's head. In green felt-tip. The Non-Wash-Offable kind.

Those sorts of things could happen to anybody.

They just happened to have happened to Martha.

Martha flung open her bedroom door. Martha waded through her piles of toys. Martha threw herself on the bed.

She would not go down, she decided. She would *wait* for them to come to *her*. Let them grovel! Let them apologise! Let them bring her peace-offerings of hot chocolate with marshmallows on top.

Martha waited.

Not long now, she thought. She could almost smell that hot chocolate wafting up the stairs.

Nobody came.

They didn't care if she died of thirst! Her own family! They were down there stuffing themselves with goodies, and they didn't care one bit about her.

It was just typical, that's what it was.

Martha found a soggy banana under her bed, and chewed on it, pondering about the Unfairness of Life.

Martha reckoned most people were unfair. Especially parents and sisters. Yet whenever she complained about this they would just say, "Life is unfair. Get used to it." Martha did not see why she should get used to it.

People were always telling children what to do. Especially Martha. And when she complained they said, "You are only a child, Martha. You have to do what you are told." Martha did not see why she should do as she was told.

Her brother, Baby Boris, never did what *he* was told. Nobody minded. They didn't shout at him, or stop his pocket money, or say he was "the worst child I've ever met". But when Martha pointed this out, they just said, "Boris is only a baby, Martha!" And when she, Martha, did the same as Boris, and slept when she wanted, and woke up when she wanted, and weed and pooed when she wanted...well.

Let's just say it wasn't fair what happened next.

If only *she* were Boss of the Universe, thought Martha. Everything would work much better than it did now.

* * *

Downstairs Martha's family were discussing her.

"She's impossible!" groaned Dad, slapping his hand against his forehead in a despairing gesture. Then: "Ow," he said quietly. "That hurt."

Mum said, "Maybe it's just a phase she's going through."

Mum believed in looking on the bright side.

"Some phase!" said Dad. "She's been like this since she was born."

"Now that's not true," said Mum.

"Oh yes it is. Do you remember when she was a little baby? She had just grown her first tooth? And we took her to that Christmas Party?"

"N-no," lied Mum. She did remember really. She was just trying not to.

"She bit Father Christmas, that's what she did," said Dad. "Six months old and she's snapping at Father Christmas like a baby crocodile!"

"*I* remember," said Martha's sister Sally.

She wasn't supposed to be part of the conversation but she had a way of butting in. "And then he wouldn't give *me* a present either. It wasn't my fault. I'd been good as gold all year." Sally was always good as gold. Gooder, if possible.

"And since then it's been downhill all the way," said Dad.

"I wish," said Mum wistfully, "there was something we could do! If only there was somebody we could call for help. Just like you might call the Exterminator to sort out a hornets' nest in the attic. Or to kill the rats. Or a plumber for a nasty smell in your kitchen. If only there was somebody who dealt with dreadful children!"

"Now you're just being fanciful," said Dad. "Anyway, nobody would take on Martha. They would have to have" – he waved his arms – "Interstellar Powers! More than that! They'd have to be a Magician! Even then they wouldn't manage it. They'd be too scared to try."

He would have been astonished had he known that somebody was listening to him. Somebody a very long way from Planet Earth. Somebody who did have Interstellar Powers (including interstellar hearing). Somebody who wasn't scared to sort out Martha Bones.

Oh yes. Martha was about to get a big surprise.

* * *

A very, very long way from Martha's home there was an office.

On the office door there was a sign.

How To Make Bad Children Good

Do you need Pest Control?

So you know how to deal with rats and mice. Now let us deal with the two-legged kind. Give us a call and before you know it your irksome infant will be everybody's favourite child!

No more being banned from restaurants! No more dreading the school report. No more pretending that your wretched child is actually somebody else's. Or being tempted to leave them behind on a bus or train.

Our trained Guardian Agents will:
Reform the Revolting
Neutralise Naggers
Tame Terrors
Ameliorate the Amazingly Anti-Social
Mollify Monsters

Or Your Money Back – Guaranteed.

Fred paused at the door to read the sign. "Money Back Guarantee," he muttered. "But we don't ask for money." It was not that kind of Agency.

Fred knew about the Agency because he worked for it. Or at least, he used to. He had just had a very long break from work because...well, because he was so bad at it. But now his boss, Archie, wanted to see him.

Rather nervously, Fred opened the door and went in.

"Ah, there you are, Fred," said Archie, looking up and frowning over his spectacles. "Come in."

Fred edged in and sat down on a small, floating cushion.

"Err, what happened to the clouds?" he said. "They were comfy." He looked at Archie. "And the halos? And the feathery wings?"

"We have to move with the times," said Archie sternly. He looked hard at Fred. The air shimmered, and suddenly Fred was dressed just like Archie: in a shimmery silver and purple robe, and with a sparkly purple glow round his head.

"Hey!" said Fred, taken by surprise.

"You'll get used to it," said Archie. "I've left your wings," he added kindly, "as you're used to them."

Fred ruffled his feathers. He *was* glad to keep his wings – even if they were a bit drab and moulting in places. But he wasn't sure about the new clothes.

And all that purple!

"You're going to have to get your act together, Fred," said Archie sternly. "Now that you're an Interstellar Agent."

"An Interstellar Wots-It?" asked Fred.

"An Interstellar *Agent*," said Archie sternly. "It's what we're called these days. You'll soon get used to it."

He brought up Fred's file on a shiny screen that floated in the air between them.

FREDERICUS ANGELICUS

WORK NAME:	FRED
CATEGORY:	INTERSTELLAR AGENT (4th CLASS)
JOB DESCRIPTION:	MAKING BAD CHILDREN GOOD (OR AT LEAST, BETTER. OR AT LEAST, NOT ANY WORSE THAN THEY ARE ALREADY)
PERFORMANCE RECORD:	POOR
PROMOTION PROSPECTS:	EXTREMELY POOR
SKILLS:	FLYING 3/10

SKILLS (cont'd):	SINGING	4/10
	NAVIGATION	6/10
	ETHICS AND MORAL	
	JUDGEMENT	5/10
	EMPATHY FOR	
	CHILDREN	1/10

NOTABLE	
PAST CASES:	ATTILLA THE HUN,
	SHERIFF OF
	NOTTINGHAM, SNOW
	WHITE'S STEPMOTHER
	(NOTE: FRED SAYS THAT
	WAS JUST A FAIRY TALE),
	HENRY VIII.

NOTES:	POOR TRACK RECORD.
	HAS BEEN "RESTING".
	A NEW CHALLENGE
	MIGHT HELP HIM TO
	GAIN CONFIDENCE AND
	FINALLY GET PROMOTED
	TO THIRD CLASS.

"You didn't do very well with your last child, did you?" said Archie, looking through Fred's file.

"Well...he did grow up to be England's most famous king," said Fred. "Henry VIII – everyone knows about him."

"Yes - because he chopped his wives' heads off!"

"Only two of them," said Fred quickly. "Two wives out of six. That makes four wives whose heads he *didn't* chop off!"

Archie tutted and shook his head. Fred sighed. It was true, King Henry VIII had not been a great success.

"Well, you've had time to get over that now, so I've decided to give you another job."

"Oh no!" squeaked Fred. "I mean – actually, I *am* still getting over it. I'm still trying to work out how I could do better next time!"

Archie inspected his watch. It had a special hand for centuries, as well as one for years, and months. "You've had *five hundred years*," he pointed out. "How much more time do you need?"

"Err – can I have another hundred?"

"No!"

"Fifty?"

"No!"

"How about two days?"

"Certainly not. You are starting work immediately. I've a lovely, dear little child who badly needs a helping hand."

"Oh," said Fred weakly, "*lovely* is she?"

"Well...no, she isn't lovely yet," Archie admitted. "Otherwise she wouldn't need our help. But I'm sure she will be lovely soon. When you've given her a few pointers."

Fred tried not to groan. He knew there was no point arguing.

"Take this," added Archie, producing a suitcase from under his desk. "It's got a few little extras to help you do the job. Gizmos we've come up with during the last five hundred years. And here's her file."

Fred mumbled his thanks and shuffled towards the door.

He had hoped that Archie had forgotten all about him. Or even decided to give up on him altogether. But that was the trouble. Archie was too good at his job to give up on anybody. Even a hopeless case like Fred. Even though Fred was just about the worst Guardian Agent that the *How To Make Bad Children Good* Agency had ever had.

At the door he turned around. He opened his mouth. He almost told Archie his terrible secret... the one he had never told anybody.

But he couldn't. Instead he walked quietly out of the door.

"Martha Bones," muttered Fred, looking at the file. "Wonder what she's like?"

INTERSTELLAR CHAT

Archie to Fred:

By the way, forgot to say, I'm going to be expecting regular reports from you, Fred. We've got this special Interstellar Chat Line set up now – don't think we had it last time you were posted to Earth. You'll soon get the hang of it.

Fred to Archie:

Is Tthere a Handbook Too say which butToijns to prenss? Whalt was rong with pen aNd ink anwyway?

Archie to Fred:

Got to move with the times, Fred. Have fun!

CHAPTER TWO
Ill Met By Moonlight

Fred arrived onto the bed post with only the slightest thud.

Not a bad landing, really. Given that it was so long since he had been on Earth.

And given that Earth's atmosphere was so different from what he was used to. And given that he had never been good at landing anyway.

"Not bad, Fred," he said. "Not bad at all."

He looked round the room. It wasn't what he had expected. Obviously things had changed a lot since the sixteenth century.

Still, one thing he noticed immediately, it was very clean. And tidy. There were lots of books, arranged very neatly. Some stuffed toys sitting in a line. A clarinet, and a music stand.

The girl, fast asleep in bed, looked neat too. She had blonde plaits and blue striped pyjamas. She was smiling as she dreamed about getting full marks in her maths test the next day.

"Well!" said Fred. "She doesn't look so bad..."

He was feeling a lot more cheerful.

He went floating about the room, taking a closer look at all the Prizes for Good Work, the

Awards for Excellent Conduct, the beaming photos, the First Class Certificates for Music, Ballet, Neatness, Handwriting...really, he thought, Archie must have decided to be kind to him after all!

Her homework was neatly set out on her desk. All of it labelled Sally J. Bones...

Oh no. Fred blushed. How embarrassing! He had got the wrong child!

* * *

Five seconds later he landed in Martha's bedroom.

This time he missed the bed post altogether and crash-landed on the rug. He got himself up. Then he looked around.

What a mess! Martha's toys were everywhere. Lots of them were broken.

And there were mounds of clothes and books and felt-tip pens without lids on.

And old crisp packets and dried-up modelling clay and her rock collection and biscuit crumbs and old banana skins and the string of her kite which ended up wound round Fred's foot. He had to use his Interstellar Powers to untangle it. Then he floated up onto the bed post to take a look at Martha.

There wasn't much to see. Only a hump of duvet, with some grubby-looking feet sticking out one end, and a few curls of hair at the other.

Fred coughed. Then he coughed louder.

"Awake," he said. The hump snored on.

"Awake, child," he said more loudly.

Nothing.

"WAKE UP, YOU STINKER!!!" he bawled.

Martha uncurled. Her head poked out from under the duvet, like a tortoise from its shell. Then she bounced up and her blue eyes fixed on Fred.

"Who are *you*?" she demanded. "And what are you doing in *my* bedroom?"

Fred bowed. "Greetings, dear child. My name is Fred and I am your new Guardian Agent! With my help, and a lot of hard work, you are about to become a better child."

Fred beamed. Martha narrowed her eyes.

"I don't believe you," she said. "It's a trick. You're not a Guardian Agent – whatever that is. You're a burglar."

"I am *not* a burglar," said Fred. He was really offended. "I mean, do I *look* like a burglar?"

"You look like a mess," said Martha.

Actually, he did. There hadn't been time to iron his robe before setting off, or to polish his halo – or rather, the purple glowing thing he now had instead of a halo. Travelling through space had made his hair even more windswept than usual and his glasses were squint.

"And how many Interstellar Agents have you met, may I ask?"

"*Interstellar* Agents? Not many," Martha admitted. "Well, not *any* I suppose."

"Exactly!" said Fred.

Martha rubbed her nose. He couldn't be an Interstellar Agent. Could he? But then again she didn't think he was a burglar either. For one thing, he hadn't set off the burglar alarm, and her parents always set it, every single night. For another there were the wings. Burglars did not have wings.

"What is an Interstellar Wots-It anyway?" she asked. A sudden thought came to her, and she grinned. "I must be very special to get one!"

"I suppose that's one way of looking at it," said Fred. "Though it's not so much a matter of *special* as - well, as..."

"As what?" asked Martha.

"As *bad*."

Another silence. "What do you mean?" asked Martha.

"Bad," said Fred impatiently. "You know. Horrible. Obnoxious. Disgusting. Awful. Revolting. Repulsive. That sort of thing. You're *all* of them. And I'm here to make you GOOD."

Martha stared. Her face grew redder and redder. Her eyes narrowed. Little crackles were coming off her, like electric sparks. Fred began to feel alarmed.

"You see, I work for the *Make Bad Children Good* Agency," he gabbled, trying to distract her. "Someone has to do it. I mean everyone knows *parents* aren't up to the job. Ho ho! They're no use at all. So when it all gets too much, when we hear a cry for help, we step in. Or fly in. Some people used to call us Guardian Angels but it's all gone a bit more hi-tech since I was last on the job. I expect it's the same for Fairy Godmothers too – they're probably zipping around on transporter beams or solar-powered rockets –"

Martha was not listening.

"NOOOOOO!" she wailed. It was such a horrible noise that Fred froze in mid sentence. "That's the last thing I need! Someone else bossing me around. I've already got Mum and Dad and Sally and Mrs Humphreys and Miss Bussy at school all nagging me...and what none of them understand," said Martha, "is that I am ABSOLUTELY PERFECT AS I AM!"

"Oh no, you're not," said Fred.

"Oh yes, I am!"

"Oh no, you're not. You're not even nearly perfect. You're not even *Shows Promise* or *Just Needs a Nudge in the Right Direction Now and Then*. In fact, you are what we Interstellar Agents call –" He paused for effect.

"Well?" asked Martha.

"– A STINKER!"

"Oh!" gasped Martha. She grabbed the nearest thing – it was One-Eyed Rabbit – and hurled it like a boomerang at Fred.

Fred was ready for her. He swooped behind the wardrobe door. Then he called out: "And I would have you know that STINKER is one of the worst kinds of child there is. It says so in my Handbook."

HOW TO MAKE BAD CHILDREN GOOD AGENCY HANDBOOK

page 13

BAD CHILDREN: Main Categories

01.   Scamps – not so bad
02.   Scallywags – worse
03.   Brats – thoroughly unpleasant
04.   Prats – don't ask
05.   Little Monkeys – nastier than they sound
06.   Terrors – obnoxious
07.   Rats – even more obnoxious
08.   Rascals – avoid if possible
09.   Rapscallions – irritating mainly
10.   Stinkers – Watch Out!

"I am not BAD," Martha said. "I am MISUNDERSTOOD. And I don't *want* an...

an Interstellar Wots-It or whatever you call yourself! So you can just...flap off!"

For a moment Fred was shocked. Then he said, "Now that's proof that you're a Stinker. You don't even *want* to get better."

"Because there's nothing wrong with me!"

"Is that what everyone else thinks?"

"Yes!" said Martha. After all everyone thought she was wonderful *really*. Didn't they?

Fred raised his eyebrows. Then he opened a big folder.

"Let's see...'You are one in a million, Martha' – your Dad said that only yesterday."

"He meant it in a good way."

"Then why did he groan when he said it?"

Martha was silent.

"'You are so repellent you remind me of a squashed bug on my shoe.' That was your sister Sally two days ago –"

"Well, you can't trust anything *she* says!"

"And then Miss Bussy: *"Martha has been really trying this term."*"

"Children are *supposed* to try at school."

"They are not supposed to try their teachers' patience to the point of a nervous breakdown!" Fred shook his head. "No, there's no getting away from it. They all think you're a right pain in the posterior!"

"What's a posterior?" asked Martha.

"Your bum," said Fred.

"That's rude!"

"Interstellar Agents are never rude," said Fred loftily. "Unlike Stinkers." He waved the file. "Oh yes, it's all written down here."

NAME:	MARTHA BONES
CATEGORY:	STINKER.
AMBITIONS	
IN LIFE:	"TO BE AN ONLY CHILD"
	"TO BE A RICH AND
	FAMOUS INVENTOR
	AND NOT GIVE MEAN
	FAMILY ANY MONEY"
NEEDS:	IMPROVING IN
	EVERY WAY
FAULTS:	SELFISH
	MEAN
	ENVIOUS
	SULKY
	RUDE
	DISOBEDIENT
	HOT-TEMPERED

CONTINUE OVER PAGE -

"Well I don't care!"

"If it makes you feel any better, *I'm* not over the moon either," said Fred. "A Stinker's the last thing *I* need."

"Then let's forget the whole thing."

"If only we could." He heaved a sigh. "But my boss won't let me. He's very stern, you know. I can't just walk away – or fly away, even." He shook his head. "No. I'm afraid we're stuck with each other."

Martha did not agree. And Martha did not take things lying down. (Or even sitting up.)

She thought of hurling herself at Fred like a human cannonball. But then she might hurt herself.

She thought of hurling her mug of bed-time hot chocolate at him instead. There was only one problem. Her cruel, neglectful parents hadn't *brought* her any bed-time hot chocolate.

So instead she opened her mouth as wide as it would go and SCREAMED.

Martha had powerful lungs. Her teacher always said that if the school fire alarm ever broke Martha could take over. Her Dad always said that Martha could have a great career playing werewolves in horror films.

"YAHHHHHHHHH........!" she screamed.

Her parents burst through the door. They were shaking.

They thought there must be a tornado or an earthquake or a volcano or that the house was burning down *at the very least*.

"What is it?" cried Mum.

"What's the matter?" yelled Dad.

"Get him out of here!" shrieked Martha.

"Who?"

"Him! That Interstellar Wots-It!"

Martha pointed. Her parents looked.

"But there's nothing there," they said.

Martha stared. It was true. There was no sign of Fred. Not even a feather.

"He was there a moment ago! *He was*."

"Just a silly-billy dream," said Mum soothingly. "You silly sausage you." She gave Martha a kiss.

"Geddoff!" said Martha. "He was *there*, you donkeys!"

Of course, they did not believe her. But they did not stop to argue. They rushed off to look after Baby Boris, who had woken and was howling like a banshee.

Left alone, Martha did not know what to think. Was Fred real? Or wasn't he? She really wanted to know.

INTERSTELLAR CHAT

Fred to Archie:
    Right. Got the hang of this chatting business now.

Archie to Fred:
    So how did you get on?

Fred to Archie:
    I've met her, the dear little girl, it all went very well, couldn't
    have been better...

Archie to Fred:
    That's excellent news!

Fred to Archie:
    Can't you tell I'm joking? She's terrible, horrible, repulsive!
    Please, please let me off!

Archie to Fred:
    Now that is not the attitude.

Fred to Archie:
    It's my attitude!

How (not) to Make Bad Children Good

Archie to Fred:
   Remember, children are like delicate, budding plants. They just need a little nurturing...

Fred to Archie:
   Plants, you say? Then this one's a cactus!

Chapter Three
A Bad Start

Martha woke up. She looked round the room. She looked under her bed. She looked in her wardrobe.

Nothing.

"Good," she said loudly. "It *was* a dream. I thought so. Interstellar Agent! As if an Interstellar Agent would look like that... *overgrown parrot!*"

She clattered downstairs, three at a time.

"It's me!" she yelled, bursting into the kitchen. "Me! Me! Me! Me! ME!"

Nobody answered.

Mum was feeding Baby Boris toast. Or rather, she was *trying* to feed him toast. "Cutchy-coo," she murmured. "Does ducky little Baby Boris like his toasty-toasty yum-yums?"

Boris was throwing the toast on the floor and laughing.

Dad was working on his brand-new laptop.

Sally was eating cornflakes *without* slurping.

Martha sat down. How boring it all was! She kicked Sally under the table, just to liven things up. When everything had calmed down again ("It was an accident!" shrieked Martha. "You horrid brat," yelled Sally), Martha decided she too would have cornflakes for breakfast.

There were no cornflakes left. Just a very few crumbs at the very bottom of the packet.

Suddenly Martha knew she wanted cornflakes more than anything else in the world.

"It's not fair," she shrieked. "I want cornflakes!"

"Try some toast," said her mother. "Little Boris likes toast, don't you darling... oh sweetie-pie, don't throw it on the floor again!"

"It's not fair that Sally finished them," said Martha.

"Oh yes, it is," said Sally smugly. "*I* was up bright and early. So I deserve the cornflakes. If only you had been up bright and early, instead of lounging about in bed! They're really delicious," she added, somehow managing to crunch the cornflakes, and smirk at Martha, both at the same time.

Martha thought about seizing Sally's cornflakes and hurling them to the floor. But that would have been a waste of cornflakes.

Instead, she waited until Sally went to get some orange juice from the fridge. Then she grabbed Sally's cornflakes and began shovelling them into her mouth.

"Hey! Those are mine!" Sally yelled.

Martha shovelled faster.

"Give them me!"

Sally lunged for the bowl. Martha held on tight. For a moment there was a cornflakes tug-of-war.

Sally was bigger.

Sally was stronger.

Sally was bound to win...

Martha couldn't stand for that. So Martha did a very wicked thing. She deliberately...*let go*.

Sally staggered backwards. A tidal wave of cornflakes came hurtling after her. SPLASH. The cornflakes hit Sally. THUD. Sally landed on the floor - in the middle of a pool of cornflakes.

"Oh no!" Sally howled. "My bum's all soggy!"

Mum and Dad were furious with Martha.

"You could have splashed my laptop!" yelled Dad.

"You could have splashed darling Boris!" yelled Mum.

Dad rushed out to get a towel for his laptop, even though it wasn't wet. Mum and Sally rushed out to get a towel for Sally, who was. Baby Boris and Martha looked at each other, and chuckled.

And then, suddenly, there was Fred. Sitting on the back of Mum's chair.

"*Not* a very good start to the morning," he said.

"Eek," spluttered Martha. "It's you!"

"It's me. I've been watching you." He shook his head. "*Look* at the trouble you've caused. And you haven't even finished breakfast."

"I thought you were a dream," said Martha. "A *bad* dream."

"I just wish I was," said Fred.

"Now look," said Martha. "This is silly. I don't want to be made good. I happen to think I'm very nice as I am. So you may as well just flap off and find some other child to bother."

"You won't be happy until you *do* change," said Fred.

"Says who?" asked Martha rudely.

"Says me. Because while you're bad, mean and unkind, you can't know true happiness." He took a big book from under his wing and waved it at her. "It says so right here, in the Interstellar Agent Handbook."

"Phooey," said Martha.

Fred drew himself up. "You're full of rude remarks today. *Overgrown Parrot*. Don't think I didn't hear you with my super-powerful Interstellar hearing. Well, I'm going to fix you, Martha Bones."

"How?"

"The first step is," Fred took a deep breath, "you are going to perform An Act of Kindness."

"A what?"

"An Act of Kindness. I suppose," said Fred sarcastically, "you do actually know what *kindness* means?"

"Yeah," said Martha. "I know. But I'm not doing

it. So there."

"You won't have any fun until you do," said Fred. "I can promise you that!"

"You're wrong," Martha told him. "It's Saturday. And Saturday is the one day I *do* have fun, you old feather duster!"

"We'll see." Fred smiled an annoying smile: as if he knew something she didn't. Then he began to fade. It was like the Cheshire Cat in *Alice in Wonderland*. First his feet disappeared. Then the rest of him went hazy, until finally all that was left was the annoying smile.

While he was disappearing, Mum and Dad came back. Mum sat on Fred. (Or what was left of Fred.) She didn't even notice. She was too busy telling off Martha.

"Martha you have not been very helpful this morning," Mum began. She paused. "And do listen when I'm speaking to you!"

"I am listening," said Martha. But she wasn't listening, because it is almost impossible to really listen to somebody who has a disembodied smile hovering over their left shoulder.

"Now I've got lots to do today —" Mum went on.

"And I've got work to finish," Dad added.

"And your Dad's got work to finish —"

"And your Mum's got lots to do today —"

"And I've got lots to — I've already said that,

Tom!"

"Oh. Sorry. Well, anyway, the point is – Martha? Are you listening?"

"Yes," Martha said. And she was. Fred's smile had vanished at last.

"Now I'm going to get my hair cut," said Mum. "I'll take Boris with me. You can stay here with Dad. OK?"

"OK," said Martha. "What shall we do, Dad? Have some fun?"

"*Fun?*" said Dad. He gave a hollow laugh. "No. I've got work to do."

"But Dad –"

"*And* I've got a very important homework report," said Sally, in a very important voice.

"Didn't want to play with you anyway," muttered Martha.

"You can play quietly in your room, Martha," said Mum. "Until I get back. And then we'll all do something together."

"Like going to the ice-rink?" suggested Martha hopefully. "Like swimming? Or bowling? Or eating donuts?"

"Like...grocery shopping."

"But that's not fun!" shrieked Martha. "And it's Saturday! Saturday is supposed to be FUN!"

She stormed out, slamming the door behind her.

INTERSTELLAR CHAT

Archie to Fred:
> So how's it going, Fred? Any progress to report?

Fred to Archie:
> Give me a chance, Archie! Please. But I'll tell you this. You remember I said she was like a cactus?

Archie to Fred:
> Ahah! Changed your mind have you?

Fred to Archie:
> Yes. She's not a cactus...POISON IVY! That's what she's like. Just thinking about her brings me out in a rash!

Chapter Four
Jamal

Martha had a feeling that Fred would come looking for her if she went to her bedroom. So she decided to make things difficult for him, and went outside instead.

She mooched around the garden, thinking what a no-fun garden it was. No trampoline. No swimming pool. Just Mum's boring vegetable patch and a few useless flowers and a swing that was too small. Then she noticed somebody looking at her over the hedge.

It was Jamal, the boy who had recently moved in next door. Martha did not know him very well.

"How did you get up there?" she demanded.

"I have a new fort," said Jamal. "Come and see."

"OK," said Martha. She squeezed through the gap in the hedge and into Jamal's garden.

"Wow," said Martha, gazing around her. "You have a lot of stuff."

Jamal had all the stuff that Martha would have loved but didn't have. Well – not a swimming pool. But he had everything else.

He had a trampoline, bigger than any trampoline Martha had ever seen.

He had a climbing wall with ropes.

He had a pond with stepping stones and goldfish.

He had a tree house in the shape of a pirate ship.

He had a Multi Activity Play System.

And he had a Fort. It had battlements and walkways and rope ladders and everything.

"Good, isn't it?" said Jamal. "It's an early birthday present. My actual birthday's not till next week. Of course, I'll be getting *lots* more presents then." He climbed onto the trampoline. "You can come to my party, if you like."

Martha considered. On the one hand, she liked birthday parties. And *in a way* she liked the idea of being friends with Jamal and going to his party and playing with his stuff.

On the other hand, Jamal had so much stuff that she didn't. It gave her a nasty feeling inside. Why didn't Martha have all this great stuff? Why didn't her mean, selfish parents buy it for her?

And *that* made her feel like saying she wasn't going to his birthday party after all.

Only...she did like birthday parties.

"Humph!" said Martha.

Then she had a more cheerful thought. "Still, I suppose you have to share all this with your brothers and sisters."

"Nope," said Jamal. "And d'you know why? Because I don't *have* any brothers and sisters. That's why."

No brothers and sisters! No Sally the Smug! No Boris the Brat! Now Martha had just one feeling: pure, raging JEALOUSY!

"I don't want brothers and sisters," said Jamal. "And I'm getting a guinea pig for my birthday."

This was even worse. Martha longed for a pet. Her parents told her that she had Baby Boris instead. Huh! Martha would have swapped Boris for a guinea pig any day. Or even a goldfish.

But she wasn't going to admit how she felt.

"Huh – who wants a pet?" said Martha.

"I do." Jamal climbed onto his trampoline. "I like pets. My guinea pig will be company for my rabbits –" BOUNCE!

"And my dwarf hamsters." BOUNCE!

"And my parakeet." BOUNCE!

"And my –"

Martha interrupted. "Well I'm getting a *cat* for my birthday," she said. (This was actually a lie.) "A ferocious Tasmanian bob-cat. I expect my cat will eat your guinea pig."

"Then I'll get a dog that eats your cat."

"Then I'll get a – a – a –" Martha was stumped. But only for a moment. "Then I'll get a *racehorse* to trample your dog."

Jamal stopped bouncing. He stared at Martha with his mouth wide open. "*A racehorse?*"

"Yes," said Martha.

"But where will you keep it?"

"In my garden."

"But there's not enough room."

"There will be," said Martha, "when we've knocked down Dad's shed."

Jamal looked round his garden. He wondered if he could fit in a racehorse. The trouble was, what with the trampoline, the pond, the fort, the climbing wall, and the Multi Activity Play System there wasn't much space.

For a while Jamal just bounced. Martha hummed cheerfully as she swarmed up the climbing wall.

"Well anyway," said Jamal at last, "This year we're going on holiday. On a *yacht*." His tone said *Beat that if you can.*

Martha stopped humming. Jamal was a show-off but she couldn't help it, she wanted to show off too.

She wanted to say this year she was going camel-trekking in the Sahara. Or dog-sledding on the North Pole. Or staying in a hotel with fifteen swimming pools.

But it was no good. Jamal would soon find out that she was only going to visit Granny, who didn't even live by the sea.

She took a flying leap off the climbing wall, and accidentally-on-purpose went swooshing into Jamal. He fell backwards off the trampoline, and landed on the grass with Martha on top of him.

"Oops-a-daisy," said Martha, getting up and brushing herself off.

"Watch it!" bleated Jamal, his mouth full of grass.

"I'd better go home now," said Martha. "Anyway, I think yachts are rubbish. I mean, what if you fell in?"

"I can swim," said Jamal. I've got certificates and everything."

"Yeah," said Martha. "But can you swim *faster*?"

"Faster than what?"

"Faster than the *sharks*," said Martha.

* * *

Martha whistled as she squeezed through the hedge and back into her own garden.

"I won't go!" she heard Jamal yelling in the distance. "I WON'T! I WON'T! I WON'T!"

"But there *aren't* any sharks!" his father bellowed.

Martha grinned.

Then she caught sight of Fred. He was perched on top of a small apple tree, shaking his head at her.

"Oh dear, oh dear," said Fred. "A shocking display of envy, mendacity and aggression. And all in one conversation! Why do you have to be so horrible?"

Martha didn't answer. She wondered what *mendacity* meant, but decided not to ask. She was pretty sure it wasn't complimentary.

Maybe Fred could read her thoughts.

"*Mendacity* means lying," Fred told her, "just in case you didn't know. Which you didn't, of course."

"I *did* know!"

"Liar!"

"I am not a liar!"

"Oh really? Knocking down your father's shed... for a *racehorse*. I wasn't born yesterday you know."

Martha kicked grass. She muttered something about "Bossy Old Interstellar Wots-Its Who Are Always Sticking Their Big Noses Into Other People's Business".

"It's my job to stick my big nose into your business," said Fred. "I expect you thought you'd given me the slip. But I've got this special Interstellar Agent Radar." He tapped a little antenna that was attached to one ear. "It was in the goody bag Archie gave me. Wonderful. Means I can home in on you whenever I want."

"Oh," said Martha, coldly. "Big deal. Good-bye."

"Not so fast!" shouted Fred. "How about this Act of Kindness? Have you forgotten?"

"I haven't forgotten. I'm just not doing it, that's all."

She stalked off towards the house. Suddenly she spun round on her heel.

"Just say I *did* do it," she said. "An Act of Kindness. What's in it for me?"

"For you? There's nothing in it for you. Acts of Kindness are their own reward."

"Some reward!" Martha considered. Then she said craftily, "Tell you what. We'll do a deal. Say I do something really kind. Would you arrange something fun for me? Like – like Dad taking me to the Ice Rink?"

Fred sighed. It wasn't right of course. People were supposed to be kind because...well, because kindness was a Good Thing. Not because they were *bribed* to be kind. He knew Archie would not approve. On the other hand, he couldn't see how else he was going to make the Stinker change her mind.

"I suppose," he mused, "just this once. Just to get you started. Just until you get the idea."

"You're on!" Martha cried. She ran for the house.

INTERSTELLAR CHAT

Fred to Archie:
> So she's agreed to be kind. Well, to try to be kind. Personally I'll believe it when I see it.

Archie to Fred:
> Now, now. Don't be so negative, Fred. Kindness comes naturally to children.

Fred to Archie:
> Are we thinking about the same creatures?

Archie:
> Of course. Dear little lambs...

Fred to Archie:
> Little lambs! Sabre-toothed tigers are more like it!

Chapter Five
An Act of Kindness

Martha went into the kitchen. Sally was sitting at the table, typing away on Dad's new laptop.

TAP. TAP. DRAG. CLICK. CLICK.

"Does Dad know you're using his laptop?" asked Martha jealously.

"Yes. He said I could use it while he has his shower. It's for this extremely important homework report I'm doing. All about children from other countries."

"Can I have a go?"

"No," said Sally, curling her lip. "That's *completely* different. You're not allowed to touch it."

Martha was about to wallop Sally. Just in time, she remembered about being kind.

"Can I help *you*, then?" Martha asked, in the sweetest, most sugary voice she could manage. (It wasn't a voice she used very much.)

"You?" said Sally. "*You?*" She stopped typing. She curled her lip.

"Yes, there must be something I can do to help."

"Actually there is one thing I suppose –"

"What's that?"

"GO AWAY!"

Martha narrowed her eyes. It was hard being kind to Sally. Very hard. And she was not sure Sally deserved it.

Only there wasn't anybody else. Dad was taking his shower. Mum and Boris were still at the hairdressers. It was Sally or nobody.

Sally hummed happily as she went back to her homework. She had forgotten all about Martha. What a wonderful homework report! It was almost finished too. How clever she was! She was sure to get the best marks in the school. Maybe she would even win a special prize...

She did not notice Martha moving about the kitchen. She did not notice the clunks and clatters. She did not even notice the horrible, burning smell wafting around the room.

"Surprise!" yelled Martha. She shoved some burnt toast under Sally's nose.

This, Sally *did* notice.

"Eeek!" she squeaked and joggled Martha. The toast almost landed on Dad's laptop. Sally grabbed it just in time.

"What d'you think you're doing?" she squealed.

"I've made you a lovely, tasty snack."

"*Lovely*? It smells disgusting. And you could have ruined my homework."

"It's not disgusting. It's delicious. It's my new invention," went on Martha proudly. "Mashed sardines with marmite and a layer of strawberry jam. On toast."

Sally shuddered. Then she threw the toast in the sink. Then she ran into the hall yelling, "Dad, Martha's being a pain!"

Martha shook her head. So this was her reward for all her trouble! This was what came of doing an Act of Kindness! Sally Snot-Nose getting her into trouble again.

She looked at Dad's laptop. Why was Sally allowed to use it when she wasn't? It wasn't fair.

She sat down and quickly typed SNOTNOSE at the top of Sally's report.

Hah! That would show her.

She pressed some more buttons and made the report turn pink.

Yes!

She pressed some more buttons.

Fabulous! All the letters had turned into squiggles that Martha did not recognise at all.

She pressed yet more buttons.

This time, one of them was Delete.

Presto! The screen went blank.

Martha looked again. The screen really *was* empty. Martha pushed some more buttons but Sally's report did not come back. All her Dad's work had vanished too. What had she done?

Serves her right, thought Martha. But she felt

a bit nervous all the same.

"What are you doing?"

Sally was back. Martha tried to stand in front of the laptop so her sister couldn't see it. But it was no good.

Sally pushed Martha out of the way. At the same moment, Dad came in wearing a bathrobe.

Martha decided to make a quick exit into the garden. Only she couldn't. Mum and Boris were coming in through the back door.

She was trapped.

"Look what she's done!" shrieked Sally. "It's vanished! My whole report has gone. My wonderful report. Oh no. OH NO! OH NOOOOOOO........."

* * *

Martha was sprawled on her bed reading a comic when Fred flew in. This time he crashed-landed on the rug, before bouncing off the wardrobe.

"That must have hurt," said Martha.

"We Interstellar Agents are invincible," said Fred, rubbing his nose. "Almost invincible, anyway. But you might give me a hand up."

Martha gave him a hand up.

"You aren't a very good flyer, are you?" she said.

"I'm just a little out of practice," said Fred,

with dignity. "That wardrobe took me by surprise. Anyway, I'm better at flying than some people are at Acts of Kindness."

"I *was* kind," said Martha indignantly. "I made Sally a nourishing snack. And then I helped her with her homework."

"*Helped her with her homework*! Ruined her homework, you mean! All gone with the click of a button!" Fred shook his head. "Mind you, these computers are silly inventions. What was wrong with paper and ink? *That* didn't vanish with the click of a button!"

"So it wasn't my fault?" asked Martha hopefully.

"It *was* your fault," said Fred. He frowned at Martha. Maybe she would learn from this, he thought. Maybe she would become humble and apologetic. Although, come to think of it, she didn't look apologetic. In fact...she was grinning.

"I'm looking forward to going ice-skating," said Martha.

"Ice-skating!" Fred gave a hollow laugh. "Who do you think you're fooling? As if anyone is going to take you ice-skating! As if -"

At that moment Dad stuck his head round the door. "Martha? Are you ready?" He didn't notice Fred.

"Yes, Dad," said Martha, jumping up.

"Remember to wear something warm – it'll be

cold at the rink."

The door shut.

Fred stared from the door to Martha and back again.

"But -" he bleated. "But -"

"Sally was so upset about her homework that Mum and Dad decided she needed a treat," said Martha. "And they can't leave me at home. Besides, Dad was so relieved that I hadn't destroyed his work, that he's forgiven me. He thought I had at first. But it turns out I just changed it into Cantonese." She got to her feet. "So we're all going ice-skating. Good, isn't it?"

She winked.

"But, but –"

"After all, it's only fair. I *did* do an Act of Kindness."

"No, you didn't!"

"Oh yes, I did. Think about Sally's teacher! She won't have to read that boring report." Martha skipped towards the door.

"You're impossible!" Fred yelped.

Martha paused with her hand on the door handle. "Funny," she said. "That's what Mum and Dad say too."

INTERSTELLAR CHAT

Fred to Archie:
> I DEMAND a transfer. I absolutely insist. Today I asked her to do a Little Act of Kindness, and what happened? She destroyed her sister's work and then got rewarded – by going ice-skating.

Archie to Fred:
> Well...

Fred to Archie:
> Her parents weren't even that cross. They said they hadn't been doing enough as a family recently, and it was good to have a refreshing break at the ice-rink. Even her sister wasn't that upset in the end. She had to redo her homework– but then she likes doing homework.

Archie to Fred:
> So why are you complaining?

Fred to Archie:
> Because – because – BECAUSE! That's why!

Chapter Six
Jamal's Birthday

"Isn't it nice of Jamal to invite you to his birthday party," said Mum, trying to brush Martha's hair.

"He just wants to show off his presents," said Martha, dodging under Mum's elbow.

Martha and Jamal had become friends – of a sort. The sort that are always squabbling, fighting, showing off and being rude to each other. Their families were never sure if the two liked each other – or hated each other. Neither were Martha and Jamal.

Still, Martha was looking forward to the party. It was bound to be fantastic. There had been no expense spared. And the food – her tummy rumbled just thinking about it.

"That's a lovely gift you've got for him," Mum said.

"No it isn't," said Martha. "I got two for Christmas, and I hate them."

Martha was stomping up the path to Jamal's house when Fred appeared. He hovered in the air just above Martha's head.

"What do *you* want?" Martha grumped.

"Now, now," said Fred. "I'm just here to help."

"How?" asked Martha suspiciously.

"You're not looking forward to this party, are you?"

"I am," said Martha. "At least," she added, "I'm looking forward to the food. And the games. And the magician. And the party bags. But –"

"But?" Fred asked.

"It's the presents," Martha grumbled. "He's sure to get loads of great presents. And he does show off."

"Why can't you be happy for him?"

Martha sighed. "I suppose I might be happy...if I had great stuff too."

"Just as I thought," said Fred, nodding. "What we have here is a case of the Green-Eyed Monster."

"What!" Martha nearly jumped out of her skin. "You mean there's a monster round here now, too? Isn't an Interstellar Wots-It enough?" And she peered over her shoulder, expecting to see the monster appear at any moment.

"No, no." Fred chuckled. "The Green-Eyed Monster is what people call Envy."

"Envy?"

"Yes. You know. Envy. Jealousy. Like when you grudge Jamal his nice things and wish you had them instead."

"Oh."

"A very nasty feeling, Envy. A definite vice. But I,"

said Fred proudly, "have thought of a way to help you. Yes, you need never envy Jamal again."

"What, really?"

"Yes, really."

Martha's face lit up. "You mean – you mean you're going to give me lots of great presents too? Oh wow!"

"Err – well – no," said Fred. "That's not what I meant."

But Martha wasn't listening. "Oooh!" she squeaked. "Goody! I'd like a dog and two guinea pigs and a trampoline bigger than Jamal's and three rabbits and my own fort and –"

"STOP!" Fred held up a hand. "I did *not* mean I was giving you loads of stuff."

"Then what *did* you mean?"

Fred took a large green bottle and a spoon from out of his sleeve. "*This.*"

"What is it?"

"Medicine," said Fred. "Drink up!"

Martha thought she would much rather be given a guinea pig than swallow some bright green medicine. But obviously Interstellar Agents had their ways. For although she meant to fight him tooth and nail, instead she found herself gulping down a large spoonful.

Actually, it tasted nice.

"Mmm!" she said, licking her lips. "Lime and

Chocolate and Peppermint all mixed up! And that's going to stop me feeling envious?"

"Oh no. It won't change the way you *feel*."

"Then what is it going to do?"

"It'll help train you," Fred explained. "You've heard of turning green with envy, haven't you?"

"Yes," said Martha. "But –"

"Every time you feel envious, and *especially* if you say something mean as a result, you'll turn green."

"What!" shrieked Martha.

"A lovely, bright, emerald green! From top to toe! Like a lizard!"

"But I don't want to turn green!"

"Then no mean remarks," said Fred. And he vanished.

* * *

Martha rang Jamal's door bell. There was a banner on the door with "HAPPY BIRTHDAY DEAR JAMAL" in enormous gold letters. Martha scowled at it and wondered if anyone would notice if she pulled it down and hid it in a bush.

"Hey Martha!" said Jamal, opening the door. "You're the first."

"Happy Birthday," growled Martha. She handed him his present.

Jamal ripped the paper off at once.

"My Own Little Flower Press," he read off the box. "Hours of fun for every wildflower lover."

"Lovely, isn't it?" said Martha. She was feeling more cheerful again. "I just knew you'd like it."

"Mmm. It's something I haven't already got, I suppose."

"Yes, and you can squash lots of things in it besides flowers," said Martha encouragingly. "I tried to squash Boris's finger, but Mum caught me."

Jamal tossed the flower press to one side. "Come and see my other presents," he said. "They're great."

Jamal showed Martha his new guinea pigs with their silky fur and snuffly noses.

He showed her his skateboard that made racing car noises.

He showed her his racing car that did skateboard tricks.

He showed her his knight's castle made entirely out of chocolate, *and* his hot air balloon kit *and* the saxophone *and* the Make Your Own Fireworks kit.

He showed her the triple-layer chocolate-toffee birthday cake with flashing lights that sang "Happy Birthday to You".

And all the time Jamal was waiting. He was waiting for Martha to make a rude remark. He was waiting for her to say the cake was rubbish, the skateboard silly and the castle sure to melt. He was waiting for her to say she was getting much better stuff for *her* birthday.

The ruder she was, the better. That way, he would know she really *loved* his stuff...admired it, envied it, LONGED for it. And then Jamal would be happy, safe in the knowledge that he really had been given some great stuff for his birthday.

But she didn't.

She just made a funny face like she was sucking on a lemon and then said, in a sickly voice that did not sound anything like Martha, "Lovely!" or "How nice!" or "You must be ever so pleased!"

Jamal began to get worried. What was *wrong* with his stuff? What was wrong with Martha? Why wasn't she being horrible?

He threw himself onto a chair and slumped.

Now it was Martha's turn to feel surprised. Why was Jamal looking so miserable? It was his birthday! And he had all this lovely loot! And she had been nice about it, too.

As an experiment she said, "Lovely presents, Jamal."

Jamal grunted.

"*Dear* little guinea pigs."

Jamal shrugged.

"That castle looks pretty good – if you like that

kind of thing."

Jamal sighed.

Funny, thought Martha. *What's the matter with him?*

"So, is that all of it?" she demanded.

"There is one more thing," muttered Jamal.

He'd been saving the best for last. He'd reckoned Martha would be stunned and amazed when she saw it. He'd reckoned she'd burst with shock and envy. In fact he'd been looking forward to it all day. But now – if she just looked bored and said, "Isn't that nice?" in a polite voice – well, he reckoned *he'd* be the one to burst.

Reluctantly, he beckoned Martha to follow him.

Martha gasped.

Standing next to Jamal's wardrobe – in fact, *towering* over Jamal's wardrobe – was...was...

Tyrannosaurus Rex. Yes: scary, toothy, growling, flesh-eating Mr T-Rex himself. Not actually live and breathing, but if you didn't know T-Rex had been extinct for 65 million years you might have wondered. It was *huge*. OK, not as huge as the T-Rex Martha had seen in the Natural History Museum one time, but still three times as big as Martha. Its teeth were pointy, its eyes were mean and when Jamal pushed the secret button it leaned forward, opened its mouth and ROARED!

Martha nearly wet herself.

It was the most amazing thing she had ever seen in her life. Oh, how she wanted it! She wanted it more than anything! She'd set it on Sally. She'd terrify Mum. She'd pulverise Boris! She'd introduce it to Miss Bussy somehow. Oh, she could do a thousand terrible things...if only it were hers.

She opened her mouth. She tried to make herself say *"How nice, Jamal, you must be pleased"* in a bored sort of voice. She tried to yawn. But she couldn't. She just couldn't.

"It's rubbish!" she squeaked. "Call that a dinosaur? It wouldn't frighten a flea!"

Jamal stared at her. Slowly his mouth curled up in a huge grin.

"I knew you'd love it!" he yelled.

Martha had a sudden thought. She looked down at her hand. But it was OK. She might be feeling mean and envious – she might have said a mean and envious thing – but she wasn't turning green.

Now, why was that? she wondered.

* * *

Fred was not pleased when he called in later that evening.

"I don't know," he grumbled. "You were doing so well. Then everything went wrong."

"Then why didn't I turn green?" Martha asked him. She was very curious about this.

"You certainly deserved to."

"Well, I may have made the odd mean remark –"

"The *odd* mean remark! You said his cake tasted stale and his guinea pigs were bald…"

"Well, once I started being mean, I thought I might as well go on," Martha explained. "And do you know what? Jamal likes it better that way. He was much happier when I was mean than when I was nice."

"Oh, you think so, do you?"

"Yes. Every time I said something mean, he gave a big grin. The meaner I was, the happier he got. In fact, I bet you right now he's saying to his Mum and Dad, '*Do you know what, that was the best birthday I ever had!*'"

Fred groaned.

"It's true!" he moaned. "And that's why I couldn't turn you green. He loved it. And that *is* exactly what he's saying at this moment!"

INTERSTELLAR CHAT

Fred to Archie:
> I don't understand it. Envy is a bad thing, isn't it? And when people act mean and envious, it makes other people unhappy, doesn't it?

Archie to Fred:
> Of course. You shouldn't have to ask.

Fred to Archie:
> Well, not this time. The meaner Martha was, the more her friend liked it! I meant to turn her green in punishment but – well, I just couldn't!

Archie to Fred:
> Ah, you see: little girls are sweet creatures really. Sweet as sugar…it says so in the Interstellar Handbook.

Fred to Archie:
> Well, the Handbook got it wrong! She's sour as limes! And inside she's as green as limes too.

Chapter Seven
Children Who Want

Fred flew round and round the chimney pot of Martha's house. He was thinking about what a rough time he was having, and how unfair it all was.

It was raining. Fred could have used his special powers to project an Interstellar Weather Shield – or at least to produce an umbrella – but he didn't. He didn't care about the raindrops dripping from his nose. He didn't care that his robe was soggy. Being soggy suited his miserable mood.

He had never asked to work with children. If a mum couldn't sort out a difficult child, or a dad or a grandma or a granddad or a teacher...then why should *he* be able to? Just because he was an Interstellar Agent. OK, he could fly. So what?

The terrible truth...the terrible secret he had never told anyone...was he didn't even *like* children! Well, why should he like them? Horrid little beasts!

Humans should sort out their own young. That's what Fred thought. He would tell Archie so, too, if... if...well, if only he were brave enough.

Fred sniffed sadly. He was scared of Archie. And he had a feeling that if he, Fred, didn't do better soon, he was going to be in real hot water. He wondered what Archie would do to him. He might tell Fred off...he might cancel his holidays...if he were really angry he might even *fire* Fred. Then Fred wouldn't be an Interstellar Agent any more. That would be...well (Fred thought about it for a few moments) actually, that might be rather nice.

Fred stopped in mid-air and almost collided with a seagull. It gave him a look. *Will you please leave the rooftops to us birds*, its expression said. Fred ignored it.

He was going to get himself fired!

"What a wonderful idea!" he declared. "Fred, you are a genius! Take a pat on the back!"

He was so pleased with his plan that he forgot to flap his wings, which meant that he fell onto the roof with a thump.

The seagull shook its head at him and sighed.

* * *

It was Children in Want Week at Martha's School. This meant that all the kind and thoughtful students were spending a lot of time thinking about children less fortunate than themselves.

They wrote poems about them.

They donated toys to them.

They were planning a raffle and a sponsored run and a dress-up day to raise money for them.

Miss Bussy, the Head Teacher, said it was wonderful to see how much the children in the school cared about others less fortunate than themselves, and what wonderfully kind, generous children they were.

She obviously hadn't been speaking to Martha.

"I don't see why we have to do all these things for *other* children," grumbled Martha, as she walked home with Sally and Mum in the rain. "Children we don't even know."

"Now that's not very generous," Mum told her.

Sally tossed her head. "Well, I'm very glad to have a chance to help children less fortunate than me. After all, I've lots to be grateful for."

"And I've lots to be *Ungrateful* for," said Martha. "Like you, for instance. Having you for a sister is a real pain."

Sally ignored this. "As soon as I get home," she said, "I'm opening my piggy bank and giving all the money to Children In Want."

"As soon as *I* get home I'm hiding all my money," Martha said. Not that Martha had much money. But that 27p was hers, all hers!

"That's not very generous, Martha," said Mum. Martha wished Mum would stop saying that.

"I'm a Child In Want too," she pointed out. "Because there's lots of things I want. And nobody ever gives them me."

"Watch out for that puddle," said Mum, a moment too late. "What things do you want?"

"New boots," said Martha, squelching her way out of the puddle. "Ones without holes in."

Mum laughed, as if Martha had made a good joke. "Well, if that's all you want –"

"It's not *all* I want," said Martha indignantly. Honestly, she thought, she hadn't even started! "I want a karaoke machine and ice-skating lessons and a racehorse and my own computer and a fort like Jamal's - and a dinosaur like Jamal's, only bigger - and I want to be driven to school every day in a limo and -"

Mum wasn't even listening, Martha realised. She had stopped to chat to another mum. Typical!

Sally, unfortunately, *was* listening.

"If only you'd read my homework report," she said, "the one about children in other countries, the one that Miss Bussy said was so wonderful it was just about the best report she'd ever read –"

"If only *you* weren't such a big head," muttered Martha.

"- then you would know that you're very lucky to go to school at all. Some children don't walk to school because they don't have any school to walk to. How terrible is that?"

Martha stood stock still.

No school! NO SCHOOL!

And she was expected to feel sorry for those children?

"Some children don't have homes to walk home to, either," Sally went on.

"You mean they get to sleep out?" Martha asked. "Every night!"

"That's right," said Sally.

"And never go to school?"

"Yes."

"I want to be one of those children," Martha yelled. "How do I get to be one?"

* * *

Over tea everyone kept telling Martha how lucky she was, and how grateful she should feel for all the things she had. But Martha didn't feel that way.

Especially she didn't feel grateful when Mum gave Boris the last bit of chocolate trifle - without asking Martha if *she* wanted it first. And she didn't feel lucky when her parents kept telling Sally how wonderful her poems and homework were - and how clever she was to write them - over and over again.

She felt so *unlucky* and *ungrateful* that she knocked Boris's bowl of chocolate trifle over Sally, accidentally-on-purpose. She got told off, but she didn't care.

* * *

Later that evening, Mum arrived in Martha's bedroom. She was smiling in a way that immediately made Martha suspicious.

"You know that School are collecting toys to give to Children In Want?" Mum said brightly.

"Yes," muttered Martha.

"Well, we wouldn't like to be left out, would we?"

"I don't mind," said Martha.

Mum ignored this. "So I thought that as you've got two flower presses exactly the same, you could give one of them. You don't use that doll's tea set any more either." She quickly opened Martha's toy cupboard.

"No!" squawked Martha. "Put them back!"

"Come on, Martha," said Mum. "After all, Sally's giving *five* of her toys. You don't want to be left out, do you?"

"I don't care what Miss Snooty Pants is doing!"

"Just think about the lucky child who gets your Flower Press and how much they'll enjoy it!"

"Huh!"

"After all, you don't need two the same."

"Yes I do. What if one breaks?"

"Now that's just silly," said Mum. "Why should one break?" She headed for the door, with Martha's flower press stuck under her arm.

Martha jumped up.

Her belongings were being seized! Her rights were being trampled! It was an outrage!

"No!" she shrieked, grabbing the flower press. "Mine!"

"Now, Martha," said Mum, "it's going to break if you're not careful -"

It broke. Bits of flower press flew through the air and one of the bits hit Martha's powder paint. Oops. At the same time, Mum let go of the dolls' tea set and it fell with a massive crash. The Children In Want weren't going to be wanting it any more.

"Now see what you've done!" squeaked Mum, through a cloud of yellow, red and purple paint.

"Now see what YOU'VE done!" squeaked Martha.

"I told you it would break!" yelled Mum.

"No, I told YOU!" yelled Martha.

"Get to your room!" snapped Mum.

"I'm already in my room!" snapped Martha.

Mum marched out, slamming the door behind her.

"If I'd slammed the door you'd have shouted at me!" shouted Martha. "You're always saying don't slam doors!"

There was no reply.

* * *

Fred appeared. He managed quite a good landing on the bed post.

"In trouble again?" he asked cheerfully.

Martha snorted.

"It's a bit of a mess round here," said Fred, looking about. "Mind you, at least it's colourful."

This was true. Now that the powder paint had settled, it looked like the inside of a rainbow. Or a paint factory, after an explosion.

Martha said nothing.

"Care to tell me about it?" asked Fred.

"Why should I tell you?" grumbled Martha. "I don't want another telling-off, thank you very much."

But she did tell him in the end. She had to tell someone, and there was nobody else.

Of course, he took Mum's side.

"It's important to think of other people besides yourself," he said preachily. "In fact, it is the most important thing in being a Good Person."

Martha gave him a nasty look. "Well, if it's so good for ME to think about OTHER PEOPLE then why isn't it good for OTHER PEOPLE to think about ME?"

"They do."

"No, they don't!"

"Yes, they do."

"Then why do they try and give away my things?"

Fred sighed. Why, he wondered, if Archie had to give him a Stinker, did it have to be the *argumentative* kind of Stinker?

"The trouble is you don't know enough about other children and their problems."

"I certainly do," said Martha grumpily. "They go on *and* on and on about it at school!"

Fred was tempted to just fly off and leave her to it. It might even get him fired, after all. And oh, he did so want to be fired!

But...it was his job to make her think about other people. It said so on Page 1 of the Interstellar Agent Handbook. In CAPITALS. In fact, of all the things Interstellar Agents were meant to do, that was probably the most important.

And besides, Fred thought, if he succeeded in making Martha think about others...when nobody else ever had...well, that would show Archie! He would see that Fred wasn't so rubbish after all. Fred might even get promoted! They might even give him a *nice* child – a scallywag, say, or a rascal.

Archie would be so pleased he might even let Fred retire.

And if Fred failed...well, then he might still get fired!

It was a Win: Win situation, thought Fred. Either

way he would be shot of Martha.

Fred got out his goody bag that Archie had given him. He had a bit of a rummage.

"How about we go to the cinema?" he asked.

"What?" Martha sat up, beaming. "I *love* the cinema! But they'll never let me go," she added gloomily.

"Ah, but this is *special* cinema! We don't need to go anywhere."

Fred fluttered his wings. The lights began to dim. Martha found herself sitting on a velvet sofa, that had appeared from nowhere in the middle of the room.

And it was amazing. It was probably the most amazing thing that Martha had ever seen.

There was no screen. Instead it was as if the whole room had become the screen. And Martha couldn't just *see* and *hear* what was going on. She could *feel* and *smell* it too. If it was hot and dusty, she felt hot and dusty. If it was cold and wet, she felt cold and wet. And if it was smelly and pongy – well, she could hold her nose or smell the ponginess too.

Fred was so involved in putting on the show that he forgot to pay much attention to Martha. He was too busy showing her all kinds of unfortunate children. Sad children. Hungry children. Lonely children. Frightened children. Sick children.

None of it surprised Fred, or even shocked him

very much, because he was an Interstellar Agent after all, and had seen a lot. What *did* surprise him was what he heard a moment later.

A loud sob.

"Eh? What's that?" he asked.

The Stinker was sitting there with rivers of tears running down her cheeks and dropping off her chin.

"Oh, it's terrible!" she moaned. "All those poor children! I can't bear it! Something must be done!"

Fred opened his mouth and shut it again.

"Can't you DO something?" Martha howled.

For a moment, Fred was at a loss. He was only an Interstellar Agent after all. He could fly. He could vanish and reappear at will. He had other powers too. But - he couldn't solve all the sorrows of the world.

He did the only thing he could think of, on the spur of the moment. "Here you are," he said, producing a large, red and white-spotted handkerchief from under his wing, and handing it to Martha.

"Thank you," said Martha. She mopped her face and blew her nose loudly.

"I'm sorry I can't do more," said Fred. And he was.

"I know," said Martha.

"You see," explained Fred, "I'm only an Interstellar Agent."

"Well, if you can't, then I will," said Martha. There was a glint in her eye.

INTERSTELLAR CHAT

Archie to Fred:
   So how's it going? Still struggling?

Fred to Archie:
   Have I got a surprise for you! My Stinker has gone all KIND and CARING! That's right! She worries about others! She thinks about those less fortunate than herself! And all because of me. So go stick that in your halo!

Archie to Fred:
   I'm delighted, absolutely delighted. No need to be rude, though, Fred.

Fred to Archie:
   Err, sorry, boss. Just wanted to share the glad tidings. May have got a bit carried away...

Chapter Eight
Martha The Good

Martha did not forget about Fred's cinema show. She did not forget about Children In Want.

And she did not let anybody else forget either.

"Of course, not everyone gets a good breakfast like this," she remarked mournfully over her cornflakes next morning. "*Some* children don't get breakfast at all."

And later that day: "Not everyone gets elevenses, you know."

"Not everyone gets lunch —"

"Or an afternoon snack —"

"Or sausages and mash for dinner, with cabbage (even though I don't like cabbage) and apple crumble and custard with sprinkles on the top."

Each time she said it, her family chewed their food more slowly. Somehow they weren't enjoying their meals as much as usual.

"Some children don't have a TV," Martha remarked that evening, as they sat down in front of their favourite comedy. "Some children have nothing to make them laugh."

Martha's family weren't laughing much either. After a while Dad switched off the TV. Mum fetched out some holiday brochures instead.

"*Some* children never go on holiday," said Martha.

Mum put the holiday brochures away.

After Martha went to bed, Mum said to Dad, "I do wish Martha would stop thinking so much about other children."

"But you've always said –"

"I know," said Mum. "I always said I wished she'd think about others besides herself. But I didn't realise then how hard that was going to be!"

The week passed. At school, the sponsored run was run. The dressing-up day came and went. The toy collection was collected. All that was left was the raffle.

Fred had never heard of a raffle so Martha explained it to him.

"First people give things to the school," she said. "Nice things like chocolates and hampers. Those are the raffle prizes. Each prize has a number on it. Then people buy their raffle tickets. When they have sold all the tickets, they have the draw. All the numbers drawn out of a hat win prizes. So if your ticket has a prize number, then you win a prize."

"Hmm," said Fred. He was quite interested. He wondered if Archie doled out children the same way.

"Miss Bussy says it's very important to get

good prizes," said Martha. "The better the prizes, the more tickets will be sold. And the more tickets sold, the more money raised for Children In Want."

Martha thought a lot about prizes. She even thought of giving some of her own stuff. The trouble was, to be honest, none of her stuff was that good. It was not the kind of stuff that would persuade anybody to buy a raffle ticket.

Besides, thought Martha, it wasn't *her* fault that there were children who needed help. It wasn't any child's fault. It couldn't be. It was the grown-ups who were to blame.

Martha sneaked into her parents' room.

* * *

On Thursday evening Dad picked up the phone. It was Miss Bussy.

"Oh hello, Miss Bossy – I mean Miss Bussy. What can I do for you?...Oh, I see...Well, actually, I don't see to be honest...I think you'd better have a word with my wife."

Thankfully Dad put down the phone and called to Mum, who was upstairs getting Martha into the bath.

"Can't understand a word that woman says!" whispered Dad, as Mum arrived. And he handed her the phone.

Upstairs, Martha discovered that bath-time was much more fun without Mum.

Mum never let her play Dinosaur Swamp.

Or make potions with Mum's favourite shampoo.

Or play Whirl Pools.

Or Tidal Waves.

Mum never let her make the water as hot as she liked either.

Martha made the bath hotter. Then she made it colder. Then she made it deeper...

Suddenly she heard a shout from downstairs.

"MARTHA! GET DOWN HERE!"

They sounded really angry.

Martha thought about hiding but there was nowhere to hide. Besides, she thought with surprise, she hadn't done anything bad lately. So how could she be in trouble?

She hopped out of the bath, wrapped herself in a towel and went downstairs.

Mum was waiting for her. Dad and Sally were there too, curious to find out what was going on.

"That was Miss Bussy," Mum said.

"I know," said Dad. "Couldn't understand a word!"

"She wanted," said Mum, "to thank us."

"To thank us? What for?"

"For me," Sally suggested. "Because I'm so wonderful." She preened herself.

"No," said Mum. "She wanted to thank us for donating such generous prizes for the raffle."

"Very thoughtful of her," said Dad. He paused. He thought about it. He frowned. "*What generous prizes*? We didn't *give* any generous prizes."

"Exactly," said Mum.

Everybody looked at Martha. Martha didn't like the way they looked.

"It's good to think about other people," Martha said. "People less fortunate than yourselves. Anyway, it was only stuff you didn't need."

"Like my new earrings?" said Mum. "The ones Gran brought from Paris?"

Martha flung out her arms. "You don't need new earrings. You already *have* earrings. Why do you need more the same?"

"They are not the same!" screeched Mum.

"Still, Martha meant well," said Dad. "It was a kind thought."

"I knew you'd understand," Martha told him. "That's why I gave them your new computer game."

"What!" roared Dad. Then he took deep breaths, trying to stay calm. "You gave them Alien Bodysnatchers 2?"

"Well, of course. You already have Alien Bodysnatchers 1. You don't need Alien Bodysnatchers 2 as well."

Dad's eyes began to bulge.

"Just like you didn't need that twenty pound note," Martha went on.

"What twenty pound note?"

"That twenty pound note in your wallet. You see," Martha explained, "you had another exactly the same. Like Mum said when she took my flower press, 'You don't need two the same.'"

This time Dad bared his teeth. He looked like Jamal's Tyrannosaurus Rex.

"Thank goodness you didn't take any of *my things*," said Sally.

"You didn't have anything good," said Martha. "Well, except for those gift vouchers Aunty Lena sent you. They'll make a nice prize."

She smiled round at her family. Her family did not smile back. They did not say, "Well done, Martha." They did not say, "How kind and generous." They did not say anything nice at all.

"You had no right!" thundered Dad.

"You should have asked!" shrieked Mum.

"You little brat!" squeaked Sally.

"GET TO YOUR ROOM!"

Martha opened her mouth. She was going to shout right back. But then she noticed something.

"Why is it raining in here?"

"Don't change the subject!" yelled Dad.

"But she's right," squeaked Sally. "Look!"

Everyone looked up to see where the drips were

coming from. A big bulge had appeared on the ceiling. It was like a bubble under the paper. And it was growing bigger...and bigger...until suddenly...

It burst. Hot, soapy water came pouring down on top of them.

Martha had left the bath taps running.

INTERSTELLAR CHAT

Archie to Fred:

So glad everything is going well. The dear, kind, generous child! You see, I said you would bring out her essential goodness if only you adopted the right attitude! If you go on like this, who knows – you might be ready for promotion!

Fred to Archie:

Oh, well, that is wonderful Archie! Wonderful! Err – excuse me a moment - I'll just go and see what kind, generous thing she's doing now.

Chapter Nine
Martha Leaves Home

Martha sat in her room where she had been sent in disgrace. She wasn't angry. She wasn't in a huff. (Well, she was a BIT angry, and a BIT in a huff.) But the main thing was she couldn't believe it.

It was so unfair.

It was the most unfair thing that had ever happened to her in her whole life - and that was saying something.

She had been Being Good! She had been Thinking About Other People. Just like they were always nagging her to do. How come her horrible parents didn't see it that way?

And the ceiling collapsing and all that hot water and plaster pouring down over everything – well, that was just bad luck. Besides, Martha had never liked that carpet anyway. Or that sofa. Maybe a good wash would improve them.

A tear trickled down Martha's nose.

Nobody appreciated her. Nobody loved her.

Even Fred seemed to have disappeared – just when she could have done with a chat.

She had had ENOUGH.

She was RUNNING AWAY.

"They probably won't even notice I'm gone," she said loudly. She got up. "And if a certain Interstellar Agent decides to stick his big nose into things, then he can just SHOVE OFF!"

* * *

First she packed her bag. Just the essentials, she decided.

She opened her piggy bank. She had even less money than she thought: 11p plus a two euro coin. The two euros would be useful if she got as far as France.

Then One-Eyed Rabbit. And One-Eared Wombat to keep him company.

Her lucky rock collection. She wasn't leaving that!

Her lucky shell collection.

Her broken computer game console. And her broken mobile phone.

Her red and black-spotted Flamenco Dancer outfit that Granny and Gramps had brought back from Spain. *And* her Nurse outfit. *And* her Fireman outfit.

Her Make Your Own Fridge Magnet kit.

Then a little light reading...

Martha dragged her bag across the floor. OK, so maybe it was a bit heavy.

She shut her eyes and threw stuff out of the bag

until it was light enough to carry. Then she set off across the landing.

Sally's door was open. Sally's room was empty. Martha nipped in to see if there was anything useful she might take.

Then she set off downstairs.

BUMP! BUMP! BUMP!

"What's that noise?" demanded Dad, sticking his head into the hall. He was holding a mop.

"I'm leaving," snapped Martha.

"Ha ha," said Dad.

"I'm serious."

"Have fun," said Dad, shutting the door.

What a mean father he was, thought Martha. His own daughter was leaving home, his own flesh and blood, and he didn't even care! He was probably pleased!

In the kitchen Martha wrote a note.

> *To Hoom It May Consern*
> *I am tired of this family.*
> *I am tired of its mean ways.*
> *You dont luv me and I dont luv you.*
> *Good bye.*
> *Your dorter*
> *Martha*

Outside, it was raining.

Martha reached the garden gate. But she had forgotten her umbrella. Her favourite umbrella, with the skull and crossbones. Should she go back? But what if they caught her?

Raindrops were trickling down her neck.

Now what am I going to do? Martha thought.

She was cold.

She was wet.

She was hungry.

She wasn't sure anymore that 11p and 2 euros would get her all the way to France.

She was strictly forbidden to go out of the garden gate on her own.

"Phooey! I'm not giving up!" said Martha.

She pushed open the gate and out she went.

* * *

The water was all mopped up at last. And nobody had even noticed that Martha had run away.

Mum was bathing Boris. She squelched across the soggy bathroom floor.

Sally was doing homework. She smiled, dreaming of full marks tomorrow.

Dad was making dinner. CHOP, CHOP, CHOP went his chopping knife. Onions sizzled in the pan.

"Dinner!" yelled Dad.

The rest of the family came downstairs. They sat down. They began to eat.

It was spaghetti with meatballs. Martha's favourite. There seemed to be plenty left in the pan.

"Wait a moment," said Dad suddenly.

They all stopped chewing.

"Where's Martha?" said Dad.

They all stared at Martha's empty space.

"Sulking, I expect," said Sally.

Mum went into the hall. "Supper, Martha!" she yelled. "NOW!"

There was no answer.

"Don't make me come and get you!" yelled Mum.

Still no answer.

Mum went back to the table and sat down.

"It will be her own fault if her food is cold," she said.

Everyone went on eating. Then Dad put down his fork again. He had a funny look on his face.

"What's the matter?" asked Mum.

"It's Martha," he croaked.

"What about her?" asked Mum.

"Err..." said Dad. "I think she's run away."

"What!" yelled Mum.

"What!" yelled Sally.

"Ugah ugah!" yelled Baby Boris.

"She told me she was going," said Dad sheepishly. "But I thought she was joking." He rubbed his hair.

"Oh dear."

"What's this?" asked Sally, picking up a piece of paper.

It was Martha's note.

They read it, then they all stared at each other.

"Maybe it *is* a joke," said Mum uncertainly.

At that moment the phone rang.

DRING! DRING!

"Hello?" said Mum. "Who is this? I haven't got much time —"

"It's me," said a deep voice. "I mean —" and the voice got even deeper, "it's the police!"

"The police!" squawked Mum.

"Yes. Have you lost a little girl?"

"A little girl — you mean — is it —?"

"*Very careless*," said the voice. "You should be more careful. A lovely little girl like that. Talented, kind, good-looking. They don't grow on trees you know!"

There was a pause. Then - "*Martha*!" Mum snarled. "Is that you?"

"Is Martha the dear child's name?"

"No," snapped Mum, "but it's my horrible daughter's name all right!"

The voice tutted.

"Martha, where are you?"

"I shouldn't have thought you'd care," said Martha, and hung up.

* * *

Fred was worried. He could not find Martha anywhere.

Usually he could find her with no trouble at all. For one thing, she was so often in her room, sulking. And if she wasn't he could always use his Interstellar Radar. He had programmed it to pick up the waves of meanness and grumpiness that she gave off, so he could home in on her.

But this time those waves weren't there.

Fred began to feel *really* worried. Where was she? At this time too?

"It's not that I *like* her," he told himself. "Oh no. Certainly *not*. I mean, I don't like children! Horrid creatures! But – well, I would like to know that she's alright."

Fred flew round and round the roofs of Martha's street. He was so anxious, he almost bumped into a chimney. Then, all of a sudden –

BEEP! BEEP! went his Interstellar Radar. It was picking up something.

It wasn't grumpiness exactly. Or meanness.

Still, he really hoped that it was Martha. He tried to work out exactly where the signal was coming from.

* * *

Mum checked the caller's number. It was not the Police Station. It was Sally's mobile.

"She's got my mobile!" squeaked Sally. "She's sneaked into my room and taken it! Just wait till I get hold of her!" She rushed off to check if Martha was hiding in her room.

"She still might be using it from the Police Station," said Dad. "We'd better check."

But Martha was not in Sally's room. She was not at the Police Station either.

She had vanished.

INTERSTELLAR CHAT

Archie to Fred:

Fred – what are you up to? Your signal keeps coming and going – are you flying in circles?

Fred to Archie:

Yes. Look, I'm a bit busy at the moment. I've experienced a temporary hitch. - Oops! I've just caught my robe on a TV aerial!

Chapter Ten
Martha The Fugitive

"So here you are!" said Fred, poking his head through a gap in the holly.

"You took your time," said Martha. "It's a good hiding-place, isn't it? It's taken you ages to find me!"

Martha was sitting on a picnic rug. She was warm. She was dry. She was nibbling chocolate biscuits.

It had been a good idea to run to Jamal's.

Not that she was in Jamal's *house*. Oh no. That was the first place they would look.

She had found a secret place. It was between Jamal's fort and her own Dad's garden shed. The roof of the shed and the roof of the fort touched, but the walls did not, so there was a sheltered space in between. You could only get to it by crawling through the holly bush at the back. The holly was very prickly. Perhaps that was why Martha and Jamal had never discovered the hiding-place before.

"What are you doing here?" asked Fred.

"Running away."

"Running away! That's terrible! You must go home at once!"

"No! I won't."

"But you must!"

"Why?"

"Well, think how worried your family will be."

"Huh." Martha sniffed. "They don't care about me!"

"Of course they do!"

"No they don't! *They* think I'm a Stinker too!" A tear trickled down her nose. "Just because I flooded the house! It was only a small flood. We needed a new sofa anyway. And alright, so I gave away some stuff..."

Fred quietly handed her a handkerchief. This one was blue with a cloud pattern.

Martha wiped her eyes. "I was only trying to help!"

"Why don't you tell me the whole story?"

So she did. She had just about finished when they heard a tapping sound. It came from the wooden wall of the fort above.

"Who's there?" called Martha.

"Me!" called a voice. It sounded like Jamal.

"Password!" called Martha

"Golden-haired guinea pigs!"

"Eat too many carrots!" replied Martha. (This was the Counter Password.)

There was a piece of washing-line leading down into Martha's hiding-place. Now it began to move up into the fort.

A few minutes later it came down again. There was a basket attached to the end.

"My invention," said Martha proudly to Fred, as the basket landed beside her.

"Mine too!" yelled Jamal. "Anyway, who are you talking to?"

"Nobody," yelled Martha.

She looked in the basket. A torch. And a packet of jelly babies.

"Thanks, White Tiger," she called. (White Tiger was Jamal's code name). "Can I have something to drink?"

"Coming up, Red Leopard," yelled Jamal. (Red Leopard was Martha's code name.) There was a clatter as he jumped off the fort and ran to the house.

Meanwhile Fred had reached a decision. Without even stopping to think that this might be his best chance ever of getting fired, and that he was going to blow it, he drew himself up and said in a loud, commanding voice, "Martha. Go home!"

"Why?"

"Because I say so!"

"Bossy boots!"

"And – it's the right thing to do. You cannot run away from your troubles."

"Why not?"

"Well…" Fred tried to think of a good reason.

"It's...well...because it's wrong, that's why."

Martha screwed up her eyes. "I bet you'd run away from me, if you could. Why don't you run away from me?"

"Because Archie would catch me," said Fred.

"You see!" said Martha triumphantly.

Fred banged his fist against his head. For a moment he looked a bit like Martha's Dad. "Then do it for me," he pleaded.

"For you?"

"Yes."

"Why?"

"Because," said Fred. "Because I'm a terrible Interstellar Agent, that's why! Because I'm always being told off! Because if you don't go home then Archie will tell me off – again! Because I'm tired of being in trouble! Because my children always turn out badly! Because if you don't go home he'll give me an even worse child! Or if there aren't any worse children we'll be stuck with each other forever!"

Martha was astonished. She looked at Fred, who was now kneeling in the mud beside her.

She had never thought about Fred's side of things before. She had never thought that Interstellar Agents could get into trouble, too. She almost felt sorry for him...

Almost. Not quite.

"No," said Martha. "I'm not going to! So there!"

* * *

The sky grew darker. The moon was covered in cloud.

Mum and Dad were tired. Mum and Dad were feeling desperate. Even Sally was quite concerned.

They had searched the house.

They had searched the garden.

They had driven up and down the streets, and they had walked the neighbourhood and knocked on doors.

Nobody knew where Martha was.

There was no sign of her anywhere.

INTERSTELLAR CHAT

Archie to Fred:

Fred? Fred – where are you? Listen, I'm thinking of awarding
you a special medal for your wonderful work with your Stinker.
With a ceremony of some kind – in front of all the other Agents.
I mean she's been a little demon, but you've risen to the
challenge and found the goodness in her and I think you deserve
your reward. So what do you think...Fred...Fred? Fred!

Chapter Eleven
Surprise!

Martha had a little sleep.

When she woke it was not as warm as it had been.

In fact it was COLD.

Dampness was seeping through the picnic rug and through her jeans. Her bottom was feeling soggy.

It was dark, too.

Jamal's torch was not very strong. In fact, Martha thought the batteries were giving out.

And it was lonely. Jamal had gone to bed. There were no more passwords. No more baskets full of treats.

"Hello," said Fred suddenly in her ear.

"Where've you been?" she grumbled.

"Where you should have been," Fred scolded. "In *your* house!"

Martha pretended she wasn't interested. "So?" she asked in a bored voice. "What are they doing? Watching telly? Playing games? Gobbling up my share of dessert?"

"No," said Fred.

"And?" asked Martha.

"They're upset."

"How upset?"

Bet they're not that upset, thought Martha.

"Very upset," said Fred. "In fact, you may be a Stinker but -"

"Yes?" Martha asked.

"They want you back!"

Martha looked at Fred suspiciously. She was not sure she believed him. Her family were probably moving Boris's cot into her room at this moment. Or selling her toys on eBay. Or planning a big party to celebrate her disappearance.

Suddenly she heard sounds close by.

"MARTHA? WHERE ARE YOU?"

There were torch lights bobbing in the darkness, beyond the garden shed.

"I've got an idea," said Martha.

* * *

In the thick gloom of Martha's garden, the family went on searching.

"*Ow!*" yelled Mum, walking into a branch.

"*Eek!*" squeaked Sally, tripping over a flowerpot.

Dad came running out of the house. "Right, I've spoken to the police. They're on their way – *whoops!*" He collided with a tree and banged his elbow.

Dad said some bad words.

Boris squawked.

Sally began to cry.

"Oh, where can she be?" Mum wailed. "My Martha! My little one! Please, come home!"

They all stared around the dark and shadowy garden.

"What's that?" asked Sally suddenly. She pointed at the garden shed.

They all looked. A dark shape was just visible, on the very top.

"Is it –" Mum began.

"Martha can't climb up there herself," said Sally. "She pretends she can but she can't really. It's too high."

On top of the shed, Martha grinned. It had been good of Fred to fly her up here. He had made a big fuss about it. He had said it broke all the rules of the Interstellar Agent Handbook. He had even shown her the page. "I'm going to get a roasting from Archie," he had moaned. But he had done it in the end. And it had been such a lovely, whooshy feeling.

Martha took the washing-line she had brought with her and tied it to a nail sticking out of the roof.

"It looks –" said Mum, "it looks –"

"It looks like a gorilla," said Sally.

Martha had once seen an old Tarzan movie. She had enjoyed watching him hurtling through the jungle, on the end of his vine. Now it was her turn!

She gave a yell. It echoed through the night. She beat her chest. Then, holding tight to her washing-line, she launched herself into the air.

"Ahh--ahahahh!" she yowled.

It was not like the movie. She fell like a dead weight. Luckily, she had a soft landing.

"Ooof," said Dad as she hit him in the middle. They both collapsed onto the grass.

"Ouch!" said Dad. "My ankle! – My nose! – My finger! – My back! – but just tell me this, before I pass out from the excruciating pain, is it – can it be? –"

"Yes!" cried Martha, leaping to her feet. "It's me! I'm back! I've decided to forgive you after all!"

* * *

There was a lot of confusion.

They hugged her.

They kissed her.

They shouted at her.

They called her "precious child" and "darling girl" and said, "You horrible little monster, how could you do it?"

In fact, they didn't seem able to make up their minds.

But Martha had the feeling they weren't exactly

sorry to see her home again.

Maybe they would even treat her better in future! No harm hoping, anyway.

Finally, after her parents had made her promise never, ever to run away again, and Sally had made her promise never, ever to run away again, and then the police had turned up and made Martha promise never, ever to run away again ("All right! All right!" said Martha, "I will never run away again. Just so long as you all stop nagging me!") everyone changed into their pyjamas and dressing gowns and sat round drinking hot chocolate.

(Well, the police didn't. They had gone back to the Police Station.)

"I'm glad I came back," said Martha.

"Are you, sweetheart?" asked Mum.

"Yes – it was getting cold in the garden," said Martha.

"Well, we're glad to have you back," said Mum fondly.

Martha narrowed her eyes. She wanted to get things clear.

"So you *don't* all think I'm a Stinker?"

"You may be a Stinker," said Dad, "but you're OUR Stinker." Mum glared at him. "What?" Dad asked.

"Anyway, all little sisters are horrible," said Sally. "They can't help it. And at least you don't throw up when you're angry, like Lucy's little sister Amy does. Or eat your own snot."

"Yeuch!" said Martha, blushing slightly.

"And you make us laugh," said Mum. "Well – sometimes."

"Hmm," said Martha. "Go on, Dad," she said. "What do you like best about me?"

Dad was holding Boris on his knee.

"What I like about you –" Dad began.

"Yes?" said Martha eagerly.

"What I like best about you –"

"Go on," said Martha.

"What I like best about you, more than anything else is –"

"Well?!"

"You're toilet-trained," said Dad. He picked up Boris and made a face. "We forgot to change Boris's nappy."

Boris laughed.

"Morfa!" he squawked. "Morfa!"

Everyone stared in astonishment.

"Hey," said Martha. "He said my name. Martha. It's his very first word!"

* * *

As she was falling asleep, Martha heard someone humming from the end of the bed. "So you're still here," she muttered.

"That's right," Fred agreed.

"I guess we're stuck with each other after all."

"I guess we are," said Fred.

"Oh well," said Martha.

Fred looked down at Martha. When she was asleep, he thought, she looked almost like a normal child. Like a *nice* child.

And she was smiling.

INTERSTELLAR CHAT

Archie to Fred:

Right Fred, don't ignore me – I know you're there! And I'm very annoyed. You've made a real bodge of it, haven't you? OK, so she's home now, but that's not the point. On top of everything else, you broke the Interstellar Agent rules by taking her flying like that. This is very serious. You can plead, you can beg, but it won't change my mind.

Fred to Archie:

Are you...going to fire me?

Archie to Fred:

No. I've decided the worst punishment I can give you – is to leave you with your Stinker. See how you like that!

THE END

Look out for more great titles from Strident

Jessica Haggerthwaite: Witch Dispatcher

ISBN: 978-1-905537-30-3 (paperback, RRP £6.99)

Jessica has always planned to be a world-famous scientist one day. But now her mother has become a professional witch!

Who will take Jessica seriously now?

To stop her mother wrecking her plans (and breaking up the family), Jessica resolves to show her that no one needs to believe in magic these days. But her plans – like her mother's spells – don't always have the desired effect...

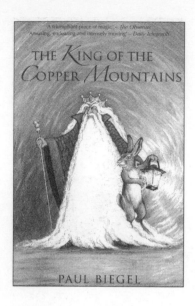

The King of the Copper Mountains

ISBN: 978-1-905537-03-7 (paperback, RRP £5.99)

At the end of his thousand-year reign of the Copper Mountains old King Mansolain is tired and his heart is slowing down. When his attendant, the Hare, consults The Wonder Doctor, he is told he must keep the King engaged in life by telling him a story every night until the Doctor can find a cure.

The search is on for a nightly story more wonderful than the last, and one by one the kingdom's inhabitants arrive with theirs; the ferocious Wolf, the lovesick Donkey, the fire-breathing, three-headed Dragon. Last to arrive is the Dwarf with four ancient books and a prophecy that the King will live for another thousand years – but only if the Wonder Doctor returns in time.

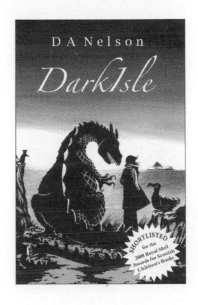

DarkIsle

ISBN: 978-1-905537-04-4 (paperback, RRP £6.99)

For 10-year-old Morag, there's nothing magical about the cellar of her cruel foster parents' home. But that's where she meets Aldiss, a talking rat, and his resourceful companion, Bertie the dodo. She jumps at the chance to run away and join them on their race against time to save their homeland from the evil warlock Devlish, who is intent on destroying it. But first, Bertie and Aldiss will need to stop bickering long enough to free the only guide who knows where to find Devlish: Shona, a dragon who's been turned to stone.

Together, these four friends begin their journey to a mysterious dark island beyond the horizon, where danger and glory await – along with clues to the disappearance of Morag's parents, whose destiny seems somehow linked to her own…

Terrifying, touching and funny, DarkIsle is a vivid and fast-paced novel of captivating originality.

Lee and the Consul Mutants

ISBN: 978-1-905537-24-2 (paperback, RRP £6.99)

The scary Consul Mutants are coming! And they're going to take over the world! Who can stop them…?

Meet Lee. Forgetful, accident-prone Lee ends up in hospital when his appendix explodes. As if that wasn't bad enough, something strange is happening. The hospital has been taken over by the mask-wearing, white-coated Consul Mutants. And they want to be the rulers of Earth!

Determined to save the planet, Lee must come up with a plan to stop the alien invasion. The world needs a hero – even if he is still at school…

Lee and the Consul Mutants is the first side-splitting Lee adventure by Keith Charters.